The Faulty Glasses
and Other Stories

The Faulty Glasses
and Other Stories

PILGRIMS BOOK HOUSE
Kathmandu ♦ Lalitpur ♦ Varanasi

The Faulty Glasses
and Other Stories

Published by
BOOK FAITH INDIA
414-416 Express Tower, Azadpur Commercial Complex,
Delhi, India 110 033

Distributed by
PILGRIMS BOOK HOUSE
P.O. Box 38, Varanasi, India
P.O. Box 3872, Kathmandu, Nepal. Fax 977-1-424943
E-mail: info@pilgrims.wlink.com.np

ISBN 81-7303-056-1

1st Edition
Copyright © 1997 Keshar Lall
All rights reserved

Edited by Judith Forrestal
Typesetting and Layout by John Snyder Jr.

Cover Design by Balaram Jana

The contents of this book may not be reproduced, stored or copied in any form--printed, electronic, photocopied or otherwise--except for excerpts used in reviews, without the written permission of the publisher.

Printed in India

Contents

Translator's Note... vii

The Faulty Glasses.. 1
The Colonel's Horse... 8
Friend... 13
The Marriage... 18
The Bet.. 23
The Soldier.. 30
Down to the Terai.. 37
A Story.. 43
The Book... 47
The School Master.. 51
The Sweater.. 58
Love... 63

Translator's Note

In the belief that Nepalese literature, especially fiction, ought to be available in English for a better understanding and appreciation of our land and peoples by our friends abroad, I have long wanted to bring out a translation of some of the popular short stories. At long last I have been able to fulfil that desire, to a small extent, by this book, which I had conceived as early as the 1970s and about which I had spoken to the author, the late Mr. B.P. Koirala. He readily granted me permission to do so. Having completed the translation, I am now very much indebted to his wife, Mrs. Sushila Koirala, for her gracious permission to publish it.

The *Doshi Chasma* (The Faulty Glasses), a collection of short stories in the Nepali language, was first published in 1950. I have translated a dozen, out of the sixteen original stories, for the present book. I have tried to be as faithful as possible to the original, both in letter and spirit. These are stories about love, that theme of eternal interest, treated from different aspects: love that is ardent or is unrequited; mystic love; love that restores sanity and brings harmony in life; and love that wrecks the very foundation of family life. Unkind, unmindful and senseless lust that masquerades as love has been treated with quaint humour. The stories also describe male chauvinism, slavish mentality, indiscretion, folly and hunger, as well as natural calamity. The stories cover the entire geographical ground in the country—the Kathmandu valley, the hills, the Terai and the Inner Terai, as well as Darjeeling, in India, where a large number of people of Nepalese origin live. In short, these are stories of great human interest.

Of greater interest is the fact that these stories were written in the late 1940s by B.P. Koirala, at the very beginning of his most distinguished career as a political leader with very strong democratic and socialist convictions and who became the first popularly elected prime minister of Nepal (1959-1960). Towards the end of his life he made a significant contribution to Nepali literature with the publication of half a dozen valuable works of fiction. Yet, by his own admission, literature was not his forte. His passion was politics of the highest order. I believe even the few stories in this book give us a glimpse of this man of great courage. He was also a man with a very large heart. Therein lies his greatness. This translation of his stories of his common fellow countrymen and countrywomen is my humble tribute to the good man.

Certain words and customs peculiar to the Nepalese context are explained in footnotes. To avoid confusing the reader with an almost identical name, I have changed one personal name in one story (The Bet). I wish to thank my friends Mr. Madhav Lal Karmacharya and Ms. Betty Woodsend for going through the translation and offering suggestions. Last, but not in the least, I thank my publisher, Mr. Rama Tiwari, but for whom this book would not have been published.

Finally, let me close this Note with the hope that, in the future, I will be able to translate *Sweta Bhairabi*, a second collection of stories by B.P. Koirala.

    Kesar Lall
    Kathmandu
    September 3, 1996

The Faulty Glasses

Keshavraj's glasses have become useless. He can no longer recognize a face from a distance. Reading has become a great strain on his eyes. He knows he needs higher powered glasses, and he had been thinking of getting himself a new pair, but he has had no opportunity so far.

He used to go daily to the general's[1] place for *chakari*[2]. One afternoon, as usual, he went but, the general didn't come even after 5.30 p.m., and all the men who had been waiting for him returned in disappointment. Only Keshavraj remained hopeful, even when the grounds in front of the gate to the general's mansion were completely deserted. It was beginning to get dark. Hidden by the hills to the west, the sun lengthened the shadows across the valley. High above in the sky, sunbeams lit up the scattered clouds. Keshavraj was fascinated by the evening scene.

Finally, concluding the general was not coming, Keshavraj made his way home. On other days, he became disappointed and sad whenever he failed to see the general, but, strangely, on this day he was light-hearted. He walked briskly along the road that skirted the field, filling his lungs with the sweet smell of the ripening rice. But his failure to

---

[1] Irrespective of whether they were in the army or in the civil service, members of the Rana family that held power in Nepal from 1874 to 1951 were given military titles. Some of them were declared generals at birth.

[2] A system in vogue during the Rana that encouraged courtiers, officials, sycophants, hangers-on and the unemployed to wait upon high-ranking members of the ruling family for the sake of personal favours and employment.

distinguish whether a black object in the distance was a rock, a log, a buffalo or a man reminded him that his glasses had become quite useless. The worry, however, did not last long, for, just at that moment, a car came honking from behind.

Because he had to know the number plate of the car in order to pay his respects to the occupant, he took hold of the frame of his glasses by the thumb and index finger of his left hand and looked closely at the plate. "Ah, these glasses have become totally useless," he muttered to himself because he could not read the number plate. The car sped past him, and only then did he recognize the car and the general in it. He made a hurried bow to the posterior part of the speeding car. He knew that his glasses had failed him. "If my glasses were powerful, I could have paid my respects properly and the general would have noticed me," he said to himself. It was a great disappointment for Keshavraj. He had been thinking for many days of having his eyes tested and of getting a new pair of glasses. For the first time he realized the importance of implementing a decision as soon as it is made. He must change his glasses; there was no doubt about it. He made up his mind to do so. If he had done so, no mistake would have been made today.

But something else worried him. It occurred to him that the general must have noticed him for he had been looking right at the car and had failed to pay his respects. It meant that he had slighted the great man, and that the general must have misconstrued his behaviour. It was also true that although he had been regularly attending upon the general's pleasure, no great favour had been done to him, and so, the general would have concluded that Keshavraj had been discourteous. Great men are apt to be very conscious of their honour, and any disrespect to them would be remembered for a long time. Keshavraj found himself in a great quandary. He was very much dependent upon the general's goodwill, and he expected great things from him. If the general misunderstood him, Keshavraj was doomed.

It became quite dark by the time Keshavraj, dwelling on such gloomy thoughts, reached home. He was beginning to get annoyed with his glasses and with himself. "What a fool I have been," he said to himself, "to open my eyes only after the mistake has been made." As soon as he entered the room, he began undressing. But the tight trousers did not come off his legs easily, and he was irritated. A moment later, when he learnt that supper was not quite ready, he lost his patience. He hurriedly climbed up the stairs to the kitchen in a bad mood. He found his wife blowing the fire with her breath to coax the wet wood that he had bought earlier that day, without looking whether it was dry or not, to flare up. "Wretch," he shouted at his wife, "you used to pride yourself at being very efficient. Yet, you are unable to feed your husband in time. What have you been doing for so long? Sitting by the fire two hours after sunset! I return home famished after business and hope to sit down to a good meal, but here you have been doing nothing...." His tirade went on.[3] His wife was not subdued by his sudden irritation, but she was indeed surprised.

Keshavraj went to bed straight after his meal, but he could not sleep through the night. He knew he had committed a great mistake. To come face to face with one's benefactor and not to pay him due respect was a crime, a veritable sin. But it was unintentional, Keshavraj concluded. He had a clear conscience because the blind cannot see, and no one can take offence from this. It was not a crime, after all. Of course, he had made a mistake, a small mistake—not to have changed his glasses in time. He had done no wrong, but the general must have misunderstood him. He must not

---

[3] A typical example of male chauvinism, which sums up the relationship between men and women among certain communities.

give the impression that he had slighted the general. But there was no remedy.

Seeing him sleepless, his wife asked, "Why can't you sleep? Tell me what is wrong with you?" Keshavraj was furious at first. Why had she to know everything concerning his affairs? But he controlled himself and said, "Oh, it's nothing." He did not expect that he could benefit much from his wife's advice in a matter of such great importance. So, he was not inclined to tell her about his problem. But when she kept insisting, he told her indirectly, "I have committed an offence. I have behaved wretchedly with a great man. To all appearances, I have slighted him. If he became angry, it would be a great misfortune. Now, what can be done?"

Keshavraj was very nervous, but his wife said simply, "Go and ask his pardon. That should put an end to the matter."

Keshavraj liked the suggestion. He decided to go the next morning to ask the general to forgive him for the lapse. The idea having caught him, he didn't want to sleep any more. In his impatience he wished it were morning at once. So, he spent the night without sleep. As soon as there was light, he put on his clothes and made ready to go out. But the hours dragged on slowly.

Three more hours had to go before it would be eight o'clock. The general would not come to the grounds until then. That was the time appointed for those who waited at his gate. Instead of waiting in his house, Keshavraj thought it would be better to go and wait at the gate itself. So at six o'clock he left his house for the general's mansion. As soon as he came out, he saw a man carrying bowls of curd in two baskets slung from a pole across his shoulders; it was an auspicious sign, and it augured well for him.

Keshavraj waited for two hours at the gate. As other people began to arrive, the grounds in front of the mansion became crowded. Downcast and alone, Keshavraj sat apart from the crowd. He thought that if he were apart from the rest of the men, he would be noticed by the great man, and he might get a chance to plead for himself and beg for pardon for his grave mistake the previous day. Otherwise, he might get lost in the crowd.

As he waited anxiously for the music of horse hoofs from within the compound walls, Keshavraj heard angry shouts instead. The general was in a bad mood.

The groom was the cause of the general's anger; otherwise, everyone knew that he was a man of peaceful disposition, none having seen or heard of his being angry before. His angry shouts could be heard outside the compound wall.

However, Keshavraj surmised that the reason for the general's temper was that his feelings must have been hurt by the incident the previous day. Of course, it was a grave matter; to touch the pride of a great man is to needle his most delicate part, something he could hardly bear. No, it would not be proper for Keshavraj to intrude at this inopportune moment, he concluded. The general's anger might fall upon him anew. Keshavraj made his way home without waiting for the general's appearance.

As he walked along, Keshavraj felt very weak. He had not eaten well nor slept at all the previous night. Overburdened by his guilty conscience, he suddenly became ill. He experienced a shortness of breath after a short while. He felt pity for himself and he was resentful that the general had actually taken offence at his small indiscretion. He said to himself: "Was it a great crime on my part? The glasses were faulty, and I didn't see well. Naturally I could not pay my respects to him. Every day I have been waiting at the gate in the morning and in the evening. If it was my intention to slight him, why would I wait at his gate? He should at least take that into consideration. If he is angry with me without valid reason, what can I do? Nothing. I cannot die." But by the time he arrived home, the train of his thoughts bogged down, and his worries returned.

"How could I behave like this when my very life depends upon him?" he asked himself, "How could an insignificant fellow like me take such a stand? It won't harm him in the least. If the misunderstanding cannot be cleared up, it will be my own ruin, and I will have to face starvation. Should we little men stand up to such great personalities? A mistake cannot be corrected by another mistake. I must go back and beg his pardon after all."

Keshavraj returned to the general's place in the evening. The general came on horseback. Keshavraj trembled all over with fear when he found himself alone with the great man, and he stammered, "Sir, the glasses were faulty. Kindly pardon me."

The general didn't understand what Keshavraj was saying. He stopped the horse and asked: "What did you say? For what do you want me to pardon you?"

Keshavraj almost fainted. He realized at once that the general was very angry, indeed, and he was not even prepared to forgive him. He saw darkness everywhere. His trembling knees gave him no support. With both hands holding his hair, he fell on the ground, a nervous wreck. The general didn't inquire further but rode away. The dust raised by the hoofs of the horse covered Keshavraj, who sat with his hands clutching his head.

He felt at once like a man of 50. He had to put his hand on his back to support himself when he walked again. He knew that he would now need a stick. His suspicions had come true. The general was, indeed, very upset with him. As soon as he came home, Keshavraj, in great distress, flung himself on the bed with his coat on. He told his wife that he would not have his supper, he has lost all appetite.

However, gradually, Keshavraj began to reassert himself. He must not give up so easily, he said to himself. He has had no chance to explain to the general. If he told him plainly, he would get his pardon. The general was full of the milk of kindness! He had only to blame himself for being unable to speak out clearly. How could he expect to be pardoned by just saying, "Pardon me." If he could explain in greater detail that it was all due to his faulty glasses that he could not distinguish the car, and that when he did, he had bowed low behind it, then there was no doubt that he would be pardoned.

The next morning Keshavraj visited the general's mansion again. He summoned courage and explained to the general what had happened from the beginning to the end. Having heard Keshavraj patiently, the general said, "Of course, I can understand the situation. Such a trifle matter! You are a very strange person."

Keshavraj recovered fully at once. The general had pardoned him. How merciful was the general! It must be because of such virtues that Laxmi, the goddess of wealth, had come to reside in his mansion and made him a happy man. If he had only said that much the previous day, he would have been spared his mental torture.

Keshavraj was very happy now.

The Colonel's Horse

The colonel loved his wife dearly. Which old man would not love a young wife? But the colonel's wife was dissatisfied with her 45-year-old husband's love; she was but 19 years old. Every time the colonel came home, he brought a present for her—a sari[4], talcum powder, rouge, bracelets, etc. However, the young woman was not happy; her mind was elsewhere, never with her husband. She usually sat alone shedding tears in the room full of things intended by her husband to please her. She had great expectations and enthusiasm when she first came to the house, but all her hopes were dashed. Whenever she thought of her past days, she sobbed. Before her marriage, a young man in the neighbourhood had fallen in love with her. A healthy man, he had strong arms, and he was pleasing to the eyes. She felt a thrill whenever she remembered him. She had rejected him for the possibility of a better man in the future. Even now, she thought of him frequently. How she would love to be securely enfolded in his strong arms! In despair, she looked around the room, and all the fancy articles scattered there seemed to hold her prisoner.

It was just at such a moment that the colonel entered the room. As usual, he had come with presents for her, clasped under his arms and in his hands. "Look, my dear," he said, "what I have brought for you." He placed before her the things he had bought.

---

[4] A woman's robe, consisting of a long piece of cotton or silk fabric which is wrapped in folds around the lower body and draped over the shoulder.

The young wife looked at the colonel and his gifts with sad eyes. "How many times have I said to you that I don't need these things," she said, wiping her tears, "Why do you waste money on these?"

The colonel said lovingly, "You are always so sad. It's the time for you to enjoy life—to eat well and to dress nicely. Tell me what is troubling you?"

The wife knew it was useless to give any answer. He would never understand her problem. A 45-year-old husband would scarcely understand the mind of a 19-year-old woman. The colonel gently lifted his wife, and momentarily she forgot her sorrow and her husband's age and threw herself bodily upon him. The colonel could not stand against her weight and both of them fell down, suddenly shattering the young woman's dream. She glanced with eyes full of contempt at her husband, who lay panting on the ground after exerting himself to lift her.

On another day the colonel and his wife went together around the grounds in their compound. He had five imported cows, and they spent a long time inspecting the cowsheds. Next to the sheds was the stable; a horse began to neigh. Hearing the horse, the wife asked her husband, "You have a horse too? I didn't know that."

The colonel had been much delighted with his purchase of a white horse. He used to attend personally to the feeding and the grooming of the horse, and he rode it around every morning. But lately he had neglected the horse and not ridden it.

"Let's go and see the horse," said the colonel.

Seeing its master, the horse was pleased. It raised its hoofs and stamped the ground and neighed. Even in the dark stable, the eyes of the horse were bright. When it neighed, its nostrils flared. Around its legs, big veins coiled like serpents. The colonel's wife found the horse an exhilarating sight. She wished to touch it, but it would not let her come near. It shook its head as if to bite her. She was not frightened; rather, she was greatly attracted to the horse.

"Oh, it is a fine, strong horse, but it does not seem to get adequate care," she observed.

"I used to care much for it when I first bought it," said the colonel, "but later on I let the groom look after it. How can I look after everything myself?"

"I'll look after it now," declared the wife. "How can we depend upon the groom? I wonder whether he feeds the horse regularly. The grooms are said to steal the feed. One must look after one's own animals."

The colonel smiled but made no further comment. From the next day the colonel's young wife came to the stable when the horse was fed. In the beginning the horse did not allow her to come near, but gradually her love won over the horse. Her touch excited the horse; it lifted its head from the trough and neighed. It stamped the ground with its front hoofs, and the stable resounded with its neighing. If the flies troubled the horse, she knew it at once, and she was happy that the horse was under proper care.

The colonel, however, was not happy with the idea of his wife looking after the horse and her absorption with the task. It didn't matter if she went once or twice a day to look at the horse, he felt, but she spent the whole day in the stable. What was the need for her to feed the horse and rub it when there was a groom?

Once the colonel said to his wife: "Why do you care so much for the horse? You don't care at all to look in the kitchen, but you feel so concerned for the horse."

"I am not a *Bahuni*[5] to stay in the kitchen," she replied sharply, "I'll do what I want to do. I get some satisfaction from looking after the horse. Can't you tolerate that much?"

---

[5] Fem. of Bahun, a common term, in the hills, for a Brahmin. Because of their relative higher status in the caste system, male and female Brahmins are often employed as cooks in rich households. Rice cooked by them is eaten by members of almost all other castes.

"What are your troubles that you speak to me like this?" asked the colonel. "What disturbs your mind, and why don't you have your peace of mind unless you are looking after the horse? Don't you have a duty to me? Do you ever think of me for a moment even as you think of the horse? Indeed, your behaviour makes me jealous of the horse." He was almost in tears as he said this.

She made no reply, but with lips curled up she looked at the colonel in contempt. She loathed the very sight of the old man moved to tears. She felt it was unbecoming of him. She wanted to give him a piece of her mind, but she controlled herself and left the place.

The next time the colonel accompanied his wife to the stable, he wished to go for a ride, but the horse would not let him come near. As his wife approached it, the horse neighed. She rubbed its back, while it kept neighing and beating the ground with its hoofs to show its pleasure.

With great difficulty the colonel got on the back of the horse, but he could not control it. It raised both front legs and stood, unmoving. The colonel was, of course, an expert in riding; he did not fall down. But suddenly he was angry, and he used the whip in his hand mercilessly. The horse did not move, even then, and as the whip lashed on its back, the woman cried in anger and accused her husband of being cruel. The next moment the horse reared its rear legs, the halter slipped from the colonel's hand, and he fell flat on the ground.

In the meantime, the young woman reached the horse, and without a glance at her husband, who was lying in the dust, she began to rub the horse gently. The nostrils of the horse grew wide with anger, and it breathed heavily. The horse had triumphed; its enemy lay vanquished on the ground. The colonel's wife had no doubt now about the strength of the horse, and she was proud of it. She put her cheek lovingly against its neck and long mane. She had a sudden impulse to ride the horse. She put her foot in the stirrup and mounted it. Her husband still lay on the ground, but she enjoyed a moment of great happiness on the back of the horse. She had got even with her husband. She loved the horse even more, and, with a glance of hatred at her husband lying on the ground, she urged the horse to move, and in its delight, it gambolled and galloped off.

When she returned, the colonel was standing on his feet. There was still a dusty spot on his coat, his hair was dishevelled, and his cap lay on the ground. His wife brought the horse to a stop near him and jumped down. She slapped the horse on its back to show her gratitude to it. The horse neighed loudly. She had never known such happiness. Suddenly, two shots reverberated from the stable. For a moment the horse trembled and then fell down on the ground. The colonel's hand held the pistol, and smoke was still rising from its barrel. Blood began to flow from the horse's stomach. The young wife looked at the horse and then at her old husband. Her face went black and blue instantly. She covered it with both hands, and she, too, fell down on the ground.

friend

Chandra Kumari came to her friend greatly agitated. Seeing her in such a state, Indramaya was alarmed, and she hastened to hold Chandra Kumari. Getting the immediate support she needed, Chandra Kumari collapsed as she put her hand across Indramaya's shoulder and held onto her. Indramaya led her friend to her room and made her sit on the bed. Then she asked, "What has happened to you? Why are you so disturbed?"

Chandra Kumari drew in a long, cold breath. "My friend," she said, "I have had a very strange experience. A great fear is gnawing me. I have not had a moment of peace. As you know, I have not come to you for the last 15 days. Please pardon me, but I was caught up in a whirlpool. All these days I have been going round and round in the whirlpool. I was so dizzy."

Indramaya took her friend's left hand and began to rub it gently. Chandra Kumari was silent for a while, and then recovering herself, she said, "How am I to say it? Where to begin? Please don't mind if I sound incoherent and inconsistent. Just listen to me. I'll tell you everything. I won't hide anything.

Chandra Kumari began her tale:

A young man came and rented one of our rooms. He came on some business, and he was going to stay in Nepal[6] for 15 days only. Now, you may wonder what could have happened within these 15 days? How shall I explain it to you? How shall I describe this man and his magnetic personality? He came like a storm, greatly disturbing me. Surely, he was not an ordinary person. At the very sight of him, one is

---

[6] Since ancient times, until quite recently, the word Nepal has been used generally by most people in a restricted sense to mean the city, as well as the valley of Kathmandu.

spellbound, and there is no knowing where it will lead or how it will end.

My husband became friendly with him at once, and the man began to drop into our room without any hesitation. I even said to my husband: "How dare he enter our room? I feel uncomfortable, and I don't like him." But my husband did not heed my words. The dreadful experience began that very day.

There was but one wooden partition between our room and his. It must have been about 10 o'clock, and that witless husband of mine could not sleep. There was still light in the other room, and he went in for a chat. There was nothing I could do but listen to their conversation. They wished to smoke, and my husband called me to bring the packet of cigarettes to him.

As soon as he called me, the man said, "She must be sleeping. Why wake her up? I will fetch it." He came in immediately, and I had no time even to pretend to be asleep. He asked, "Where is the packet of cigarettes?"

In a great alarm, I reached over the pillow for the packet and held it out to him. Somehow my hand trembled, and he noticed it. Instead of taking the cigarettes, he took hold of my hand. Fool that I was, I blurted out in a low voice, "What are you doing? If he came to know it?"

He became bolder and asked, "Could I kiss you?"

I was filled with consternation. With a great effort, I made a humble request, "Leave me now, I pray. Perhaps, later..."

For a brief moment, the young man was motionless. Then a faint smile lit up his face, and he said, "All right" and went out of the room.

Back in his own room, the talk between them resumed. For a while, I was frozen with fear. When my husband came back to sleep, I asked, "When will he leave?"

"Why?" he asked.

Recklessly, I said, "I think he is not a nice person."

"Why?" my husband asked somewhat uneasily.

Taking hold of myself I said, "He enters our room without the least hesitation when we are together. What sort of behaviour is that? Just now he had come to get cigarettes."

My husband replied, "Look, you are being suspicious for nothing. He is so nice and friendly and open, and yet you suspect him."

The next day, I was going down the stairs with a pot to fetch water, and he was coming up.

He stood in my way and said, "Let me kiss you now. Yesterday you had said, 'later'."

In a cowardly manner, I said to him, "You are bent upon ruining me!"

He was very surprised by my words. He said, "Your ruin? You mean you will be ruined if I kiss you? How is that?"

I replied, "It's getting late. Please excuse me. I've to take the water upstairs quickly. Excuse me now."

He was not impressed by my words of entreaty. He asked, "How long will it take to give a quick kiss?"

All at once a feeling of hatred welled up within me. I insisted, "Will you get out of my way or shall I scream?"

In a tone of the greatest surprise, he asked, "Are you angry?"

I succumbed to him. "Later, not now," I said to him.

However bad he may be, there was something nice about him. He never tried to use force upon me. He got out of the way immediately when I said, "Later." He could have just caught hold of me and fulfilled his wish. What would have happened to me then?

I must admit, I was very much impressed by this streak in his nature. How could I say outright that he was bad?

One day my husband had gone to the bazaar. The young man was busy in his room writing something. I was also busy with my own chores—going back and forth between the bedroom and the kitchen. His room was located in between. Once, his eyes met mine. He stopped writing at once and asked, "Are you ready now?"

I didn't say a word but entered my own room and lay down upon the bed. Suddenly I felt very weak and spent. But I felt a strong urge to write to him. With a trembling hand I wrote upon a piece of paper: "You'll be going away soon. Yet you wish to kiss me. Why?"

I pushed the paper through a slit in the partition into his room. Then, with some effort, I closed my eyes tight and lay down upon my bed, although I didn't feel like sleeping at all. My heart began to beat fast, my throat became dry, and I felt as if I would suffocate.

From that moment, he behaved in a very strange way. Suddenly he became indifferent; he didn't care for me at all. He was always in his room reading or writing. Somehow, I was very angry with him. I said to myself, 'How can he do that to me? Who gave him the right to torment me?' He seemed to be always absorbed in his work.

Once or twice I even boldly entered his room. He would glance at me and return to his book. I felt he was being unjust to me. I seemed to burn within myself, reduced to ashes. I was very ashamed. Once he had been bent upon taking my honour!

One day he was busy as usual with his writing. I entered his room. He looked coldly at me, as if I were a statue, and returned to his work. I sprang at him, snatched up the exercise book and began to tear it apart. Taken by surprise, he asked, "What are you doing?" I tore his papers into shreds, and I wept and shouted, "Here they are, here—you heartless, sinful man, you faithless creature, you scoundrel! Now, keep on writing!"

With that I returned to my room and cried and cursed him until I was out of breath.

He came to me with some concern and questioned, "What has happened to you?"

"Get out!" I shouted at him with all my strength so that I was heard all over the house.

He turned away at once. I went on crying for a long time.

When my husband came home, I said to him again, "When will he go away? Tell him to leave our house."

"Did he misbehave with you?" he asked.

But how could I tell him? I simply said, "When you go out, I am afraid to stay alone with a young man in the house."

That day I felt a sudden surge of love for my husband. I tried to forget the fear that was eating me and clung to him throughout the night. From deep within me a new awareness of love welled up. I had never felt so much in love with my husband before. As I lay with my head upon his warm chest and listened to his throbbing heart, I experienced boundless happiness within me.

To tell you the truth, my friend, from that day I really began to love my husband. Now I do not feel any hatred toward that young man either. Actually I feel somehow grateful to him.

He left today, but I have been unhappy the whole day. Deep within me there is an emptiness, and my husband has gone to the bazaar and so here I am.

Something troubles me. What shall I say of the man? Good, bad or what? It is a mystery to me. A great uncertainty is eating me up.

As Chandra Kumari ended her tale, she looked with inquiring eyes at her friend Indramaya, who had listened to her in great amazement. Later, Indramaya asked herself, 'Why was Chandra Kumari so greatly agitated?'

The Marriage

Subba[7] Katak Bahadur married a 14-year-old girl[8] and brought her home!

Anyone who did not know Katak Bahadur personally would have taken no interest in the marriage. But the mention of a 14-year-old bride made me curious to know about her. The Subba must be a mature man, I surmised. I have not seen a young Subba so far. Perhaps, it was his second marriage. From his first wife, he had, perhaps, two sons. After her death, most probably, he had married this 14-year-old girl, Harimati. Perhaps, it would not make much difference for Katak Bahadur, himself a man of experience, almost an expert, as far as women were concerned. He would scarcely spare a thought for the 14-year-old girl during the daytime, when he was busy in his office, either with his pen or with his colleagues and subordinates. But for Harimati, marriage at an age when she scarcely knew what life was all about must be quite strange.

The news of Katak Bahadur's marriage revived in me the memory of a wedding I had attended before. I was with the groom's party that went to fetch the bride. We were invited to come at four o'clock, but the procession did not move until eight o'clock. We were gathered in the courtyard, ready to go, but the groom himself dallied long. He was readying himself, we were informed. Well, we said to ourselves, only once in a lifetime a man has a chance to be a groom. So, let him take his time and enjoy it. We waited for him to put on the finishing touches. I had not seen the man himself, and I wondered about him.

---

[7] In the past, the title of a civil officer.

[8] Child marriage was common in the Brahmin community in the past.

Some women from the village were also standing there, waiting to see the groom. They were curious about him, too. When you speak of a groom, you usually think of a man in his early 20s. The villagers, too, must have been expecting to see a young man. After a long time, there was a commotion at the door. "Here comes the groom," someone cried, and everyone looked towards the door. But I failed to spot the groom. All those who came out of the door were grown-up, mature men. But there was one among them in a black coat, whom I guessed was the groom. Yes, it was he. He looked like the happiest man in the world just then—his manners and speech betrayed him.

The procession started exactly at eight o'clock. The groom rode on an elephant; we walked. As I looked at the groom, I asked myself, 'Would the bride be 35 or 40 years old? Or, would she be a young girl?'

I asked a gentleman next to me, "Is this his first marriage?"

"No," he said.

"What about his first wife?"

"She is dead. That's why he is getting married again. He has two sons by his first wife. No household can run without a woman. There is no one to take care of his sons. So, he had to marry again."

Now that I knew something about the groom, my imagination ran in another direction. I thought of the bride. The groom had to run his household, he had to have a woman to look after his small children, and so he had to marry. But what about the bride who would run his house and take care of his children. She must surely be a grown-up woman. Otherwise, how would she manage the house or take care of the children? She must also have some idea about the household she was going to join, as well as about the young men she was to look after. So, I convinced myself.

At the bride's home we found ourselves amidst a festive atmosphere, and when she was about to come out of the house, I hurried towards the *mandap*[9] in the courtyard. A large crowd had already gathered there for a look at the bride. I thought that they, too, must have been expecting a bride old enough to run a household and take care of two grown-up sons. But contrary to all expectations, two or three women pushed to the *mandap* a little girl covered all over with red clothes. I was completely wrong. The sight made me sad. How could this tender young girl run a household and take care of her husband's sons? I became thoughtful about the little girl. 'How would she live in the man's house? What kind of relationship would develop between her and her husband? What would be her thoughts now?'

From that time I did not care to go to any wedding, and I lost all interest in such matters.

I began to wonder about the 14-year-old Harimati as a child wife. I don't know whether she was happy or not, but I felt some sympathy for her. She may have heard about her future husband. She may have even been pleased when her friends teased her about being married. She must have formed an idea about the man who was going to be her husband. What sort of a man must she have imagined him to be—a young man or an old one like Katak Bahadur? Or, a small boy of her own age? How must her thoughts have run? What happiness must she have thought of? That she would have plenty of good things to eat, pretty clothes to put on, riding in a palanquin to the accompaniment of a musical band? Did she imagine such happiness?

Did the girl's hope come true when she arrived at her husband's home? How did Katak Bahadur and Harimati talk to each other? I could not help but imagine a scenario.

Perhaps, on their first night together, the girl was startled when Katak Bahadur said to her, "My darling, my own

---

[9] A small, shallow pit in which the holy fire is lit. Wedding rituals are conducted around it.

queen!" Not many days ago, perhaps, she had played with some children in the neighbourhood, and a boy had been made a king and Harimati a queen. But that was a play. A big, grown-up man addressing her as in a play need not necessarily please her.

Katak Bahadur, coming close to her, may have asked, "My dear, do you love me?"

Thinking it would please him, she may have replied, "Yes."

"Kiss me, then," Katak Bahadur may have urged her. Harimati must have been puzzled.

I was puzzled, too, by the development of the scenario. Did Katak Bahadur seek a kiss from her or did he not? Did he want to kiss her as a small girl or as his wife?

Finally, moving away from Katak Bahadur, Harimati may have said, "I am feeling sleepy. Let me sleep."

"So soon?" Katak Bahadur may have asked. He may have been taken aback by her words, which did not contribute to his happiness, for he was not wanted by his 'love.' He could only say to her, "Sleep? We can sleep any time. But let us talk now about something or other."

Harimati may have felt ill at ease in her new home and even apprehensive. She must have kept silent when she found she could not go to bed, and she kept looking at her husband's face. She could not understand what Katak Bahadur was saying. Whatever she was able to make of his conversation made him seem foolish and ridiculous.

What made me imagine all these things when I heard of Katak Bahadur's marriage with a 14-year-old girl? Perhaps, the conversation between them did not go this way. His very first question to her might have been, "Child, tell me, what's your name?"

The gentle approach may have taken away what fears she had of a new man, and she may have said boldly, "Harimati."

"How much have you read?"

"I have completed the alphabets, and I have begun to read small books."

"From now on, I'll teach you. Now, you must be sleepy. Go to bed."

Katak Bahadur may have pulled a cover over Harimati as he began to pour over the household accounts.

The next morning, Katak Bahadur would have woken her and let her have her bath and her breakfast. Then, for a while, he may have let her read; he may have corrected her when she made a mistake. After that, with the books wrapped in a piece of cloth, Harimati must have gone to school as usual.

A question, however, nagged at me: 'Why Katak Bahadur had to marry after all? To have a daughter because he had none?' If this were so, he had taken a burden upon himself on the very first night of his marriage—the necessity to marry off a grown-up girl.

The Bet

It was night time, and the newly-married couple were by themselves in their bedroom. Enraptured in the unspoken new love between them, the husband wanted to keep his wife's body and soul bottled up within him forever. The wife didn't match his desire, but she wished to contain him always within her eyes.

Padma had been teasing his wife Laxmi. To forestall her retaliation, he leaped off the bed and swiftly reached a corner of the room when a pillow landed softly on his head. However, before long the innocent fun gave way to a serious argument, and the couple ended up sleeping with their backs to each other. How it began was not quite clear, but the argument became serious when Padma said, "All women are alike. They have feeble hearts that float constantly on short-lived joys. Shall I give a living example? Do you need proof?"

Laxmi protested, "There may be one or two women of that sort, but you cannot generalize and condemn all women. They are strong enough in character. Don't speak of one or two who have gone astray."

Padma calmly replied, "I am not talking of you. Nor am I treating all women with contempt because of their nature. I am only saying that such is the nature of women. What is their place in society? What is their responsibility? They are accessory to the happiness of men. They are by nature weak and without strength of character. Of course, 'without strength of character' is not exactly the way to describe it, but for want of better words I am saying so."

Laxmi's anger knew no bounds. She said loudly, "You cannot say whatever comes foremost in your mind. You must give proof of your assertion."

He replied, "I can give you the proof. That's what I have been saying all along."

The argument ended inconclusively. The husband had to give proof before his wife would accept his opinion. If he failed to prove his point, he would seek her pardon on his knees. They then discussed whom to put to the test in order to prove Padma's point.

Said Laxmi, "I'll name Janakmanjari."

"Okay with me," said her husband.

His ready acceptance of the name made her rethink. 'Perhaps she is weak and will succumb easily,' she said to herself and proposed another name. "Let it be Chanmati."

Without the least hesitation, Padma accepted Laxmi's choice.

Laxmi became dubious again. "No," she said, "Not Chanmati, either. She is a bit coquettish. I'll not trust her. Let it be Harimaya."

A moment's reflection made her unsure of Harimaya. She said, "After all, this is a bet. Perhaps Harimaya won't do."

The husband said, "Well, you seem to be coming around gradually to my own point of view. If you cannot recommend anyone among your friends, what is wrong when I say that women generally have no strength of character?"

Laxmi thought of various other young women known to her.

She was reminded of a widow—Harikrishna's wife. As soon as she had her ideal woman, she put her hand to her husband's mouth. "Keep quiet," she said. "Try to corrupt Harikrishna's widow, if you can, to prove your point."

He raised no objections to the proposed name. If he was able to prove that the widow was weak in her character, Laxmi would accept his verdict on women. If he failed, he would change his opinion on women and get down on his knees. She would then forgive him. However, she proposed a time limit. "You have to present your proof within 15 days," she insisted.

Padma responded impatiently, "All right, 15 days are enough. But you must not take offence, and don't accuse me of wrongdoing. For the next 15 days I'll do as I like. You must not look upon me with suspicion."

"That's all right with me," she agreed.

The next morning, a thin curtain seemed to hang between them when they woke. Laxmi got up quietly and began to put her clothes in order. Padma stood before the mirror and stretched his arms. She said, "Oh, you had to look at yourself as soon as you are awake, as if you want to show your great body."

"Well, am I not handsome?" asked her husband teasingly. "Don't you like me?"

She quickly stood close to him and said, "Yes, you are most handsome to me."

That made him laugh, and she also laughed for a long time.

At bedtime that night, the wife said, "One day is gone. There are only 14 days left."

"I know," he replied.

On the following morning, too, there was an uneasiness between them. She went at once to take her bath. He hesitated for some time, then washed himself, put on his clothes and went out. When he returned home, she asked pointedly, "Where did you go so early in the morning?"

"To Harikrishna's house," he replied.

Suddenly Laxmi was on the verge of tears, but she controlled herself with a great effort and only exclaimed, "Oh, that's why you made yourself look nice and prim so early in the morning!"

"Well, what else can I do? Out of 14 days, one more has gone. I have got that bet to think of."

Without another word, she made her way to the kitchen.

That night no conversation took place between them. They took to their bed in silence.

One day, Laxmi herself paid a visit to Harikrishna's widow, who made haste to receive her. "Oh, how did you happen to come today?" the widow asked. "Lost your way, did you? You have forgotten me. I have been forsaken by God and by friends alike."

The widow's bright face made Laxmi jealous. It made her think, 'She had never been so lively before. With her widowhood, she had already lost her lustre. Where did this new brightness come from?' Laxmi found her beautiful, even in widow's clothes. She was youthful again. Laxmi stood transfixed.

The widow took Laxmi by her hand and led her inside the house. Then she asked, "Why are you looking so strangely at me? What is there left in me? Even if there is anything left at all, he is already dead."

Laxmi became lost in thought. 'She was never so spirited before; she used to be such a simple soul.'

When she came home, she attempted to draw her husband out. "The widow is very pretty these days," she said, "Isn't she quite bright?"

With a morsel of food in his mouth, Padma agreed with her. "Oh, yes, she is pretty, indeed."

Laxmi was furious. That ended the conversation between them.

In the bedroom that night, Laxmi suddenly flared up. "Don't you know I need one end of the pillow too?" she almost shouted. "You want to monopolise it, or do you wish me to sleep in another bed?"

He was taken by surprise. He asked, "Why are you angry? There is enough space. Why do you have to lie at one end? The pillow is big enough for both of us, if you come a little closer."

Laxmi retorted, "I don't like to sleep close to you."

"If that is so, have the whole pillow for yourself," he said. "I don't need it."

She turned her back on him, pillowed her head upon her left arm and said, "I don't need it either."

The pillow was left to itself between them. Neither of them used it that night.

Padma visited the young widow every day. His wife, too, went to her every other day or so. One day the widow said to Laxmi, "I am so happy when you come for a visit. You cannot imagine how lonely I am. When you are with me, for the moment, I am happy again."

Laxmi said, "I come whenever I can, when I have time. He does not leave me alone for a moment."

With that, Laxmi hung her head low.

"He must love you very much," said the widow.

Laxmi just shook her head.

"The widow put her hand on her friend's shoulder and said, "There is no trusting a man. He may love his wife, but at the same time, he may also run after another woman. They are no good. But your husband is a simple soul. He won't be like that."

She lifted Laxmi's head by her chin and said, "You are fortunate!"

Laxmi saw a chance to speak out. She said, "You don't know him yet. From a distance, yes, he is nice. Only when you scratch a man and look beneath his skin, will you find him just the same, an animal, a rake."

The widow put her hand to Laxmi's mouth to stop the flow of her words and said, "Tut, Laxmi, what are you saying? You shouldn't speak so of your husband. Your husband is very good; he is a jewel of a man."

Laxmi's anger knew no bounds. She said to herself, 'Sure he would be good to her looking forward to being a bride again. A fallen woman!'

From that day, Laxmi did not go again to her friend the widow. All day long she remained sullen at home. The husband and wife no longer spoke to each other. Laxmi got irritated with no reason, and she vented her rage upon the servants.

On the fourteenth day, Laxmi was reduced to a pitiable condition. She had a hard time controlling herself. She felt as if her whole body were on fire. She was listless and went from one room to another, from the kitchen to the store and from the bedroom to the drawing room. But she had no peace of mind. Once more she made her way to the widow's house in a hurry. The widow did not seem pleased to see her. They spent some time together in silence.

Laxmi returned home in great distress. Suddenly, she found herself in a dreadful vacuum. She felt lonely and very much afraid. She trembled all over. It became very cold. She couldn't stand on her legs. She fell down upon the bed and sobbed uncontrollably. After a long time, she felt somewhat lighthearted. Then she became weak all over and finally she fell asleep.

When her husband came home, he shook her and awoke her. He asked, "Why are you sleeping at this untimely hour?"

Laxmi rubbed the sleep from her eyes. She felt somewhat relieved but, she was very subdued and unsure of herself. She no longer had a zeal for life. She had become very feeble.

At night, the husband said pointedly, "Laxmi, this is the fourteenth day."

"Yes, I know," she replied and turned her back, pretending to go to sleep. But he knew soon that she was trembling all over. He tried to make her turn towards him and asked, "Why are you sobbing, Laxmi? What has happened to you?"

That made her cry all the more. She stifled herself with the pillow. Expressing surprise, Padma asked, "Tell me, my dear, what has come over you? For no reason at all you get angry with me these days. And you behave strangely. I am very surprised at you."

She said between sobs, "Do you love me at all? Who am I to you now?"

He moved his hand gently across her back. "Laxmi, why do you speak such ill words?" he asked. "You are the very light of my life, you are my hope, my...."

"But why are you so attracted to that widow?" demanded his wife. "Why are you beginning to love her so much?"

The husband could hardly suppress a smile. "Why, didn't you give me 15 days to prove my point?" he said. "And yet you are angry with me. Didn't I say at the outset not to suspect me?"

"You don't have to be so close to her," she protested.

"But what about the bet?" he asked. "I was going to win it."

"Well, I have lost it," she conceded. "You have won the bet. I have lost. I don't need any proof."

Padma said, "Then you agree with my view about women in general?"

Laxmi responded hastily, "Yes, I agree with you."

The Soldier

Travelling alone in the hills can be very boring. Once I had to undertake a journey for a couple of days. However, I met a soldier on the way, and it made the journey very easy.

"Oh, Babu,[10] where are you bound?" someone called in a familiar tone from behind me on the trail. Looking back, I saw a soldier in uniform coming along with quick, short steps. I had heard a lot about the rudeness of soldiers. "Ilam," I responded briefly, and in an effort to shake him off, I quickened my steps. But he came close to me in no time.

"Ah," he said and smiled, disclosing a tooth covered with gold that glistened in the sun. "I am also going there," he announced lightheartedly. "So, we shall keep each other company, at least today."

He wore a black coat, an army cap and khaki pants. The top of a cheap fountain pen glittered in his coat pocket. He had a Queen Anne watch on his wrist, which appeared from beneath the sleeve of his coat whenever he raised his hand. A large, red handkerchief was tied around his neck.

"I am a soldier, but you—God forbid a lie—must be a student. No?"

I smiled and assented.

"I can tell a person by his clothes and his speech. As a matter of fact, I haven't failed, so far, in this matter. I am an illiterate, but I can sign my name in the payroll, and I can read the Ramayana.[11] This much I have learnt in the barracks. But, if I had devoted myself to books, I would have been just like you—lean, thin and yellowish."

---

[10] A respectful form of addressing a person.

[11] An Indian epic extolling the exploits of Lord Ram, who is believed to be an incarnation of God.

I began to enjoy his talk. He spoke familiarly with all and sundry on the trail, as if he knew them well. "Where are you bound for?" he asked everyone. Because of his soldierly bearing, none dared be impolite to him. Whenever an elderly woman came along, he addressed her at once as mother-in-law. And he inquired, "How is your young girl doing? Tell me, my dear mother-in-law."

My companion didn't care to know about me. He didn't find enough time to tell me about himself. So, how would he be curious about me?

"I am at the cantonment at Quetta,"[12] the soldier explained. "It is a long time since I went there. I have a wife in these hills here. She is sick most of the time and of little use. But, anyway, she gave birth to two boys. It has been quite a while since I went home, and I have no wish to return. My wife is sure to have gone with some other man. The boys, too, must have grown up. The younger one was quite promising. I wanted to give him an education, but who is going to bear the burden? My father didn't educate me, yet I am doing quite well. I have found another wife at Quetta itself. One should be happy wherever he finds himself living."

I found it quite interesting to listen to the soldier because he was frank and open. He made no attempt to hide anything. As a student given to seriousness, I asked him, "How is life in the army?"

"Ah, what a question." He was quick with his reply. "To tell you the truth, it is a very good life. We do not have the same problems you have. Enjoy life, by all means, say our officers. And so we do. I have come on furlough. There is speculation about an imminent war, and I have come to seek

---

[12] A city now in Pakistan.

recruits.[13] Really, I have already snared six fellows. A soldier lives on milk and meat. I am not actually trapping them but doing them a good turn. The country needs soldiers."

With a puff of his cigarette, he added, "To die in the battlefield is to go straight to heaven." His face became grave when he said it, as if he were reciting from the Gita.[14]

His interesting conversation made it easy walking. Just then a group of young women, carrying loads of grass on their backs, approached from the opposite direction. With a wink at me, he said, "Just see, I am going to tease them." He stepped forward and saluted them. Then, in an undertone he said something to the women.

"Tut, tut," said the women and kept going, except one, who threw the bundle of grass on the ground, and, arms akimbo, began abusing the soldier in such a rage that her body shook and her teeth were bared. My companion reacted with uncontrolled mirth, and he exclaimed, "What a termagant! I swear that she must lash her poor husband with her tongue like this all the time."

Soon after the encounter with the women, we resumed our journey. "It is very difficult to understand women," he commented. "Once I got entangled with one of them. Oh, yes..." He drew in a long breath, became as grave as a stone statue and continued to walk like an automatic machine. The sun was beginning to sink low on the other side of the mountain in front of us. I asked him with great interest, "What happened then?"

"Oh, yes, I was saying. I fell in love with a girl. I don't know how I came to love her. I spent many days happily

---

[13] Many Nepalese joined the army in India in those days. Some still do.

[14] A famous section of the Indian epic Mahabharat dealing with the duties of humans, regardless of the consequences.

with her, and one Sunday I found I had really begun to love her. It was a holiday, and as soon as it was dark, I went to her in all haste."

The soldier's breath quickened, and he exclaimed, "She had put on a blue gown that day. Oh, she looked so beautiful!"

We had come to an ascent. "Wait," he said. "I'll buy two sugar canes. There is a climb ahead. It makes the going easier if we use the cane as a walking stick. When we reach the top, it will help us to overcome our weariness, too. Don't you like the idea?"

With that, he went off and returned soon with two sugar canes. He gave me one and then continued with his story. "But that girl deceived me. She ran away with a captain. She went with him for the pretty dress that he gave her, but I assure you, she did not stay for long with the old man. That pretty girl loved to keep moving about."

I became absorbed with the soldier's story and kept quiet. Noticing my silence, he said with a smile, "I'll bet you a bottle of liquor that you are now thinking of your wife. Isn't that so? Now, don't lie to me."

After a moment's silence, I said, "Tell me, my friend, how do you feel in the battlefield with bombs, bullets and death all around you. I cannot even imagine it."

With a derisive laugh, he slapped my shoulder and replied, "That's not a place for tenderhearted people like you. As a matter of fact, I enjoy the battlefield."

Thus, we went on talking until we came to a place where we had to stop for the night. There were at least two hours of daylight left, but the sun had gone behind the hills in the west, and we heard the sound of running water. Darkness was closing in fast.

I said, "We cannot go further. We must look for a place to stay."

"Don't worry about lodging," the soldier replied. "I know every stone here. My ancestors used to live here. Just walk on ahead. I shall take you to a shop. I know the old woman there. There was a time when that old woman attracted a great many admirers. My father was one of them. Her shop was quite successful. But now even a blind eye is not turned towards her. To be frank, if she didn't have a daughter, I would not go to her now, either."

We soon came to the shop. The wooden house was old and dilapidated. The front part had fallen down, and it had to be entered with head held low. We proceeded and found the room full of smoke. The dim glow of a small kerosene lamp made it look even gloomier. Because I was feeling sleepy, the scene appeared dream-like. Two men from the hills were drinking tea and munching stale bread. They were talking loudly, and often hit the table with their palms. Smoke filled the room, the source of which was a fire burning in the corner. On it, water boiled in a kettle. An *almirah*[15] with broken glass stood against the wall and revealed an old tin of Lily brand biscuits, an empty carton of orange pekoe tea and two or three tumblers. Resting her hand on the table, a fat old woman was listening intently to the two men. She punctuated her laughter with her own comments. I followed the soldier into the room. Seeing the soldier, the old woman straightened herself and looked at him from top to toe. She then said, "Oh, how did you happen to stray here?"

"No, I have not strayed here," he said, "but where is your daughter?" He waved his hands and paced about the room as if he were master of the house.

"She is out, but should be coming soon. You have completely forgotten us!"

Just then a stoutish young woman came in and exclaimed, "Let him forget. Why should anyone remember us?"

---

[15] Anglo-Indian name for cupboard, cabinet, wardrobe or chest of drawers.

The younger woman wore a black, cotton *dhoti*[16] with a piece of dirty cloth wrapped around it. Even in the darkness of the room, the black spots on her cheeks could be seen. She was not pretty, but her youth revealed a natural beauty.

The soldier acknowledged her presence by hastening towards her. "Oh, it's you!" he said. "You may not believe this, but it was you who attracted me here. Who can forget you? As soon as I arrived, I asked your mother for you, and you came in immediately after. Do you want me to swear that I am telling nothing but the truth?"

"Enough of your talk. You speak a lot before us, but later on...." With these words the young woman stepped inside another small room, lighted a kerosene lamp and sat down upon a straw mat. The soldier sat on the threshold and began to engage her in conversation. "Now, tell me what you have brought for me," she demanded.

I was feeling quite sleepy by then, so I didn't pay much attention to their conversation. They went on talking even after everyone else had gone to sleep. The woman asked him to bring her a mirror when he returned. The soldier promised her not only a mirror, but also a *sari*. Overcome by weariness, I slept like a log.

Early the following morning, the soldier shook me to waken me. There were at least two hours of the night left, and it was very cold outside. A cold wind was blowing between the hills, and a gurgling sound came from a stream nearby. Everyone else was still asleep, but the cocks were beginning to crow. All around stood the dark hills. Because the place was very cold, no trees grew on the slopes. I woke up rubbing my eyes. The soldier said lightheartedly, "My young friend, I must bid you good bye. I have to go one way and you the other." He shook my shoulders with his hands until I began to feel pain. All sorts of thoughts came to me. I

---

[16] A long piece of cloth, worn by men and women, wrapped around the lower part of the body.

had begun to like the fellow, but he was not affected in any way. He took to his path with long strides. I stood looking at his receding figure.

I have seen many statues of soldiers slain in the battlefield, but that was the only occasion I had come across a soldier in flesh and blood.

Down To The Terai[17]

The day broke at the confluence of the Sun Koshi and Tama Koshi rivers. The Sun Koshi came from the north, flowing swiftly, while the Tama Koshi, slow and slender like a thread, came from the east to mingle with the former. Few people could cross the Sun Koshi, but anyone with steady legs crossed the Tama Koshi. The land was barren; nothing grew on either side of the rivers. The trees stood respectfully at some distance from the water.

The five people who had spent the night huddled on the bank of the river got up as soon as the first rays of the sun lit up the water. The first thought that came to all of them was, 'What am I to eat now?' They exchanged knowing glances.

The widow's eyes sought Gore, but she addressed all of them as one: "Well, what arrangements did you make about your food when you left your home? What did you expect to eat?"

All of them were rather disheartened by her words.

Bhote said, "I don't have a home."

The old man said, "Once I had a home, but now I am also homeless. But, woman, if you have a home, why did you come?"

The four men were homeless. They would become coolies, if they could find work, or if there was nothing else to do, they would become beggars. Among them, the widow with a home was like a swan among crows. As if she were Annapurna, the goddess of grain, the widow produced parched rice[18] from her bundle and gave some of it to each

---

[17] The plains, once heavily forested, that form the southern belt of Nepal. The Terai extends to India.

[18] Rice boiled in the husk, pounded flat and kept dry. It can be transported and eaten without cooking.

of them. On top of the rice she put a piece of molasses for each person. Suddenly, there was a gleam in every eye and respect for the widow in every heart. She gave some more rice from her own portion to Gore and said, "You are young and your hunger will be greater than that of others." Then, she said to all of them, "I am on my way to the Terai. I have no husband. My parents-in-law do not look kindly upon me, and a brother-in-law treats me with scant respect. I could not remain in that house without my husband."

The four men were filled with sympathy for the widow. Even if her husband had died, it was not easy to leave a place where there was plenty to eat. They were filled with a greater respect for the woman.

"Where are you going?" she asked, "I didn't see you eat anything last night. You slept without food. As I didn't have any companion, I came near you to sleep. All the night long I kept thinking of you."

Bhote was very surprised at her words. He asked, "Why did you think of us? We are nothing to you, neither husband, nor son, nor father."

The widow replied, "But you are men."

When the bellies that had been empty for a whole day and night were filled with parched rice, the men came to life and they became animated. The old man said, "Good woman, none of us has any kin. None of us has a home. There was nothing to do in these parts, so we have come in search of work. Now, from what you have said, it seems that we, too, should go down to the Terai. What do you say, friends? Shall we go to the Terai? There we can get enough to eat. Once I had been there as a porter."

Then and there they made up their minds to go down to the Terai, and the four men and a woman took the trail to the south. The old man spoke about his past. Once he had earned a lot of money, and he had owned 17 *ropni*[19] of rice

---

[19] A land measure in Kathmandu valley and in the hills, measuring 6,476 square feet.

land; but, later, things went wrong, and he was ruined. But then he was still young, and with a strap across his brow, he was able to carry loads, and he earned enough to live on. However, he couldn't do this any more. Otherwise, would he be wandering about, hungry and aimlessly? Also, it was time for him to die. It was mainly hunger that had set him wandering.

"My wish in going to the Terai is to settle down to a quiet domestic life," explained the widow. "I'll have a small farm. It is said that farming is easy there, and land is available freely. I could not stand my parents-in-law anymore. It was sad to have to live in that place after my husband's death."

Bhote and Dhane listened to the conversation of the old man and the woman with great interest, but they said nothing about themselves. Gore seemed to be tired. He came last, dragging his feet. The widow waited for Gore. When she stopped, everyone else also stopped.

When Gore caught up, the widow said, "You must be tired, Gore. The sun is very strong. Your head must be hot. Here, take this cloth and keep it on your head." Saying this, she took the white cloth from her head and put it on Gore's.

Everyone was walking once more. Notwithstanding his age, the old man walked ahead with steady steps. On either side, Bhote and Dhane kept pace with him, listening to his account of the past. The old man found them good listeners, and he made up all sorts of stories about himself. Bhote and Dhane were spellbound, and their respect for the old man grew.

The widow and Gore followed behind slowly. Gore was 25 years old and the widow 30. Gore didn't talk much; he seemed to be shy by nature. His deeply sunk cheeks revealed

---

[19] A land measure in Kathmandu valley and in the hills, measuring 6,476 square feet.

the hardships of many days. His eyes were lustreless. The widow asked him, "What will you do in the Terai?"

"I don't know," Gore replied.

"Don't you want to settle down somewhere?" asked the widow. "Don't you wish to own a farm?"

"Where is the money to come from?" Gore said.

The widow explained, "In the Terai, you can get land freely if you wish to farm. You are young enough. Establish a household. Marry and raise children. How long will you wander about like a vagabond?"

Gore listened in silence, until the widow asked him, "Don't you like women?"

He raised his eyes, looked sharply at the widow and said, "Yes, of course, why not?"

The woman took him into her confidence. "I am going to have a farm and a household of my own," she said. "But a woman cannot do it alone. A man is also needed. It occured to me that the two of us can do it. We can make a home."

Gore looked doubtfully at the widow. She asked, "Am I not suitable for you? What if I am a bit older? I have kept myself safe and in good health. No one has touched me since the death of my husband. I didn't have any children, and so I am in shape."

Gore kept looking at the woman in amazement. She continued, "Gore, for a long time I have been thinking of a family of my own. But my husband died too soon. Now it seems that my wish will die within me. Can't I bear children? But where are my children? Where is my home? Where is my man?"

Suddenly her face became dark, and she seemed to be on the verge of tears. Her face became red, and she walked silently, with downcast eyes. The two walked together in silence for a long time.

It was beginning to get dark, and it was the woman who broke the silence: "Gore, I have some jewelry and some money, as well. We'll buy land, and we'll build a house. If you become mine, it's all yours."

The old man, Bhote and Dhane had stopped, and they were sitting upon a rock at some distance. As the widow and Gore approached them, the old man asked, "Aren't we going to stop now? But shall we eat?"

Everyone looked at the woman. She said, "I've still some parched rice left. We'll have something, even if we can't have our fill."

Gore and the widow sat down, and all of them ate whatever was left of the rice. Then they laid down by the side of the trail under the open sky. Tired from their day-long walk, they were sound asleep as soon as they laid down on the ground.

With the first rays of the sun, on the following morning, the old man was wide awake, and when he began to cough, the others also got up. But Gore was not there. The widow asked in alarm, "Where is he?"

"He must have gone somewhere," the old man replied calmly. "Let's go. We don't have anything to eat now. We have to be down there by this evening. There may be something to eat there."

The widow's heart became heavy, and she was surprised at the heartlessness of the men. Shouldn't they be sorry to lose a companion? She began to gather up her things. She was suddenly alarmed to find her jewelry gone.

Everyone prepared to leave, but the woman kept looking through her little bundle. "What are you doing?" asked the old man. "Let's go, or else we won't get down to the Terai today. We'll have to sleep with hungry stomachs."

"My jewelry is gone," the widow said pathetically.

All of them stared at the widow with great surprise.

"Why were you carrying your jewelry with you?" the old man asked. "Gore must have taken it. But what is the use of crying over stolen things?"

The widow was angry with the old man. She shouted at him, "Shut up, old man! Oh, I had thought of doing so many things with my jewelry! Buy a piece of land, marry a man, build a house of my own and have a son. All my hopes have now been dashed to pieces."

With these words, the widow began to cry loudly. The old man stepped close to her, and, putting a hand gently on her shoulder, said, "Why do you cry now, good woman? Things that could be stolen have been stolen. Something will turn up in the Terai. You'll also find a husband. You'll have a home, too. Don't be so downhearted. Let's go."

The woman stood up with a vacant look and walked slowly behind the old man.

Before long they came to a pass, and the old man pointed out a vast plain that stretched as far as the eye could see.

"That's the Terai," he said. "That's where our fortune is going to be made. There we'll have enough to eat."

There was a gleam of hope in the eyes of Bhote and Dhane. Even their sunken cheeks took on a slight tinge of red. Their wrinkled faces were wreathed in smiles.

The widow, however, had lost all hope. In her declining years, she had planned to attract a young man to herself with the allure of her jewelry and money. She had hoped to make her dream from the earliest years—a small house and children—come true. Now, it was all gone, tumbled down like a house of cards. Like her companions, she, too, looked down towards the plains in the south, but there was no enthusiasm in her.

A Story

This is a story from the hoary past, when people on earth used to compete with the gods in heaven. In those days, the gods descended upon earth and sought the help of human beings to defeat the all-powerful demons. To maintain their supremacy, like the Brahmins of modern times, the gods didn't hesitate to seek all sorts of help from lesser beings. But whenever humans sought to reach the state of the gods themselves through great sacrifices and appropriate practices, it became unbearable for the gods. Various methods were employed by them to drag the successful humans down to earth, from the heights to which they had tried to rise, by renouncing all ties to society and living all alone in dense forests, spending their time in deep thought. The most successful strategy employed by the gods to frustrate the efforts of the earthlings was to dispatch celestial nymphs, famed for their beauty, and from whose charm no man could possibly escape.

It was during that period that a certain man had gone to the forests in order to acquire the knowledge that would lead him to divinity. It was his idea that a man would not acquire such knowledge as long as he remained in human society. The affection of parents, love of wife, friendships and duties towards the society, he believed, constituted a hindrance to spiritual growth. He therefore severed all connections with human society and devoted himself solely to his meditation, subsisting only on wild fruits and water from a small stream that flowed by the hermitage. While he lived thus, lost to the world, beasts of prey forgot their sanguine nature and gathered around him. Disregarding the presence of the lion, the tiger and the bear, the deer pressed close to the hermit. Lest the peace of the hermitage be disturbed, the tiger approached slowly, its head hanging low; only the deer and the hares hopped, skipped and jumped about fearlessly. The bubbling noise of the stream served to stress the silence that reigned there, and the sound of the birds was like music.

On the right bank of the stream, there was a small meadow surrounded by tall trees. There the hermit had made his hut. If there was any spot fit for holding communion with God, this was just the place for it.

In the process of his emancipation, his first step was aimed at getting away from the control imposed upon him by his own body. Thereafter, his efforts were directed at the conquest of his mind and towards the uplifting of his soul, until it became a part of God himself. In order to be the master of his own body, the hermit practiced austerity. At the height of summer, he sat by a great fire; during the coldest month, he sat in the stream with the water up to his chin. He ate less and less, until he was able to subsist without food. Freed from hunger, thirst and cold, he sat deep in thought, and, in course of time, he was able to remain motionless for months on end, lost to the world.

Thus, months went by as he practiced austerity. The seasons changed. The trees shed leaves, and the branches became bare. The leaves sprouted again, and the forest was green once more. Flowers blossomed, and gradually the fruit-laden branches touched the ground. The fruit ripened, but the hermit remained immobile. His soul now radiated heavenly light. As time went by, the light within him became brighter, and the peace and harmony within him became more intense. The grass grew tall and covered the hermit himself. The termites began to build their nest around his feet. But the hermit was unconcerned and unmoved by what went on around him. The changes without didn't touch him; the peace that he experienced within was not disturbed.

A strange heavenly light was aglow within him. His entire being—body, mind and soul—was beginning to experience an eternal joy. Was his asceticism beginning to succeed? The hermit's eyes opened by themselves, and he surveyed the scene. His very first glance fell, not upon the changes that had come over nature all around him, nor on the termites' nest that reached up to his chest, but upon a most beautiful young woman taking a bath.

When the hermit's success began to shake the throne in heaven, Indra[20] had sent his most beautiful and accomplished nymph to the hermitage. Thinking that she was alone in the wilderness, the nymph took off her clothes and played in the water. The healthy glow of her white skin was as spectacular as the snow-covered Himalayan peaks in the first rays of the morning sun.

The nymph stood in the knee-deep water. As she bent down to take the water in her cupped palms, her undraped body looked like a bright, white flower that bloomed during the night, spreading fragrance all around. Poised like twin birds ready to seize the food before them, her beautiful breasts were very alluring. It was at such a moment that the hermit's gaze fell upon the woman.

As the hermit watched the nymph gently swaying like a lotus stem in the current of the stream, he was filled with ecstasy. She was the very embodiment of joy. What was left of his senses, after such extreme austerity, revived within him, and he got up slowly. No grass had grown on the ground where he had sat. Calm and peaceful, the hermit walked up to the bathing beauty.

They entered into wedlock then and there. After their marriage in the forest, the hermit returned home.

The hermit's fame had spread far and near. Even the king of the land had made preparations to meet the hermit with a large entourage and befitting ceremonies. But when he came out of the forest married to a woman, the whole community was stunned by his great fall. Those who had assembled to welcome him turned the other way when they saw the young woman with him. The knowledgeable among them

---

[20] The mythical ruler of the gods in heaven.

concluded that Indra, alarmed by the hermit's achievements in the realms of spiritualism, must have sent the nymph down to tempt him and frustrate his efforts.

The hermit returned to a householder's life. He built a hut close to a village and took to farming to support himself and his wife like ordinary people. In course of time, they had children of their own. The couple was ever ready to help others. When a neighbour became ill, the wife hurried to nurse the patient. Whenever the villagers were called upon to do their duty at the king's court or at the cremation ground, the hermit turned farmer, now the father of two boys, also went with them. All the villagers were indebted to him for his small acts of charity and help. If they had any problem, they sought his help as if it was their privilege to demand it.

The villagers, however, never forgot his failure as a hermit. They looked upon him doubtfully, even while he built a cow shed. Whenever they saw his wife going with a pot to fetch water from the well, they said to themselves, "She must be an evil spirit to cast such a spell over him."

However, he still retained within him the peace and happiness that had come upon him suddenly during his meditation in the forest.

The Book

The flood on the Koshi River inundated the whole district. Many people were swept away by the flood, and many more died of hunger. Sickness was widespread. Some help came from the government to these helpless people. Volunteers were sent by a number of organizations to the district. I had also arrived at a village with a group of volunteers. We had taken with us quinine, chlordane, potassium permanganate, etc.

Before our departure from Varanasi,[21] we had decided upon a plan of action. Arriving in an area, we were to visit each village and distribute the medicine. Each of us had also taken along what we needed for ourselves. I took the medicine as well as a mosquito net, but, unfortunately, I had forgotten to take my books with me.

I found the whole area under water. Some bushes appeared above the water and provided a refuge for ants, grasshoppers and other insects and worms. Wherever there was land above water, men, women and children were gathered like the ants. Sickness and hunger made these poor peasants lie down helplessly anywhere and everywhere, as if they were already on their deathbed. Some people were actually breathing their last, but those lying next to them didn't know what was happening. One man brought up whatever was inside him and just staggered to the ground. From time to time, there were cries of distress that sounded like the yelps of dying dogs. Such was the desperate situation in the places worst affected by the flood. According to a government notice, about 10,000 people died in the area.

---

[21] The ancient city in northern India, famed as a place of pilgrimage as well as an educational center for Nepalese students.

We set to work at once. First, we had to make arrangements to burn the dead bodies, then feed the living and provide medical care for the sick. We removed the dead and then separated the sick from the dying. We were able to carry some of them to the nearest village and arrange for their food and medicine. Then, we came back to those who were left along the embankments. Despite our own thirst and hunger, we devoted ourselves wholeheartedly to the task, day and night, in the belief that we were saving many lives.

In the course of time, we were able to take away the last person from the embankments. The flood had receded. The swiftness of the water was gone; it was now moving slowly, as if tired from overexertion. If we could but forget the havoc created by the flood, the expanse of water now looked as pretty as a lake. Our work was almost done, and it was about time to leave. After all the activity and excitement, the silence that prevailed now in the rural scene made us restless. There was nothing left to do, and it was very difficult to pass the time. Many volunteers had already left; only a few remained in several villages scattered around the area. Those who were left were to assemble at my place, and then all of us were to depart together.

Meanwhile, I was quite alone and idle. The rural scene was strangely calm and made a city dweller uneasy. I sat on a string cot under a *jamun* tree (*Eugenia jambos*) in the courtyard of an old peasant's home, trying hard to pass the time. A bird moved listlessly from one branch to another. The picture was one of utter loneliness and boredom. My host stood before me, with his palms joined together, and expressed his gratitude to us volunteers.

"I couldn't do anything for you," he said, "The flood swept away all my cattle, and now I have no milk nor curd."

"Don't worry," I told him, "I have had enough of everything. I'll always remember your hospitality."

But the old man went on: "It wasn't such a poor place before, but the flood has reduced us to dire straits. Otherwise, we had enough for everyone to eat and to share with visitors. Two of my milch cows were swept away in the flood. What could I do? I am old now, and it's time for me to die. But I am sad I couldn't do anything for those who came here to help. While my wife was alive, we were able to manage it, but she has gone, too."

The old man then became quiet as he made his way slowly to his hut. After a moment, he emerged from the hut and sat down at the door. Left to myself, once more I looked upwards and began to count the leaves in the *jamun* tree. I yawned and hoped that some of my friends would arrive by evening.

There was water on all sides. The sun's rays were reflected in the water, making a very boring scene. I had forgotten to bring my books, otherwise the time would have passed easily. It was my habit to take a book or two wherever I went, but I had forgotten this time. I wanted to go through Romain Rolland's *Jean Christopher,* a very popular book just then, and I had already read a few chapters. Thinking about the book reminded me of my home and made me even more restless. But what book can I expect to find in such a rural area?

In my restlessness, I stood up then sat down and laid myself on my back on the cot and made an effort to nap. The old man, staring vacantly into space from the doorway, noticed my condition, and he came near me again. "How am I to pass the day?" I asked him.

The old man replied, "There is nothing to be done. To go for a walk is out of the question. There is water everywhere. Otherwise, there are pleasant places to visit. There was a pond near that distant tree."

"It only there were a book," I said. "I could read it."

At the mention of a book, the old man's face brightened at once. "I have a book," he said. "Harihar, my son, brought it the year he died."

He went inside the hut to fetch the book. I had not expected to find an interesting one, but, even if it was an ordinary story book, I could while away the day, and by evening my friends should come.

The old man came out with something in his hand that was black with soot and resembled a book. "Harihar brought it the year he died," he said. "He was quite smart. He used to read this book. Always looking at it, he was. I had great hopes for him. But God took him early. I kept it under the rafter for memory's sake. What my son brought has come of use today."

The old man went on talking with his palms held together while I looked, with my head down, at the book he had brought for me to read. It was a catalogue of patent medicines produced by Dr. S.K. Burman (Dabur) dated 1926, listing herbal remedies for asthma, malaria, etc.

The School Master

Nandaraj set the exercise books aside and got up from his seat. It was time to take his bath, eat the morning meal and leave for school. Umanath was a good student, but the exercise books show that something must have gone wrong with him recently. It was doubtful he would pass the examination this year. He had totally forgotten grammar. Grammar teaches how to write and speak correctly. Umanath seemed not to comprehend it at all. No one can pass without a knowledge of grammar. Nandaraj scratched his head and entered the bathroom.

Emerging from the bathroom, he went to the kitchen. He ate in a hurry, put on his clothes and made himself ready for school. He had to hurry because there was little time left. It was already 10.30 a.m. 'How is it?' he said to himself, 'I never get time to eat and never get to school without undue haste. It was not Radha's fault. The moment I get to the kitchen the food is ready. I spent a long time going through the exercise books. But what could I do? I had to go through 35 exercise books in the morning and take them back to the school.'

At that moment, Umanath arrived. Nandaraj acknowledged his greetings, and putting his hand on his shoulder, said to him, "What's this, Uma? Don't you study these days? You have done it all wrong. Mind your grammar, or I'll have to fail you in the examination. If the subject is plural the verb has also to be plural. You have committed mistake after mistake. I had great hopes for you."

Umanath stood listening with his head held down. Nandaraj slapped him on his back and said, "You may go now. Study well and don't be so careless."

With these words, Nandaraj made his way to the school. 'How can I say Uma alone has made mistakes?' he thought.

'No one else is good. For the past two or three years, there has been a bad batch of students. They never pay much attention to their books. The cinema in the town has been like butter for the fire. The batch four years ago—Janardhan, Keshari, Gajaraj, Ambika—was so good. Perhaps, only that Bengali[22] boy may pass this year.'

Arriving in the school, Nandaraj entered the class room. It was a very warm day. He began to teach: "Allaudin slew Jallaludin and ascended the throne, but the situation was not very satisfactory because the pro-Jallaludin Sardars[23] were not happy with the murder...."

Many of the boys were not attentive to what he was saying. In one corner, some boys were actually laughing. Others were overcome with drowsiness, and a few were staring with sleepy eyes.

Nandaraj, however, was not discouraged. He went on with the lesson: "Having conquered all the states in the north, he cast his eyes towards the south. He sent his trusted lieutenant, Sardar Malik Quafur, to invade the countries in the south. At Devagiri, Quafur...."

But his patience was exhausted by the behaviour of the boys. He stopped in the middle of the lesson and asked a boy, "Harihar, when did Allaudin invade Gujurat?"

Harihar was startled by the sudden question. He stood up and looked with surprise at the teacher. The teacher was angry. He said, "You won't listen to what is being said in the class, nor will you study at home. How are you going to pass in the examination? If you do not wish to study, why do you come to school at all? Why do you waste your parents' money?"

Now the students were quiet. All the naughty boys turned towards the teacher with innocent faces. The teacher

---

[22] A native of Bengal, India.

[23] A military leader.

resumed the lesson: "Allaudin is very important. This may come up in the examination. Listen carefully."

The students pricked up their ears. Nandaraj continued: "No one after Ashok founded such a vast empire, but its foundation was weak."

Just then the bell rang. Nandaraj stood up at once. The students, too, rose from their seats; some stretched themselves while others yawned. For a moment there was disorder in the class. Nandaraj entered another classroom. The boys in this class seemed smart; they were quick with their answers. It was good to teach this class, but something seemed to go wrong with the boys when they advanced higher in the class. Nandaraj began the day's lesson: "A lamb was grazing near a stream. A wolf arrived there and said to the lamb, 'Why are you dirtying the water I am going to drink ?'"

All the boys had their eyes in their books. After the lesson, the teacher asked, "What is the moral of this lesson?" When a student gave a satisfactory answer, the teacher said, "Yes, never keep bad company."

Nandaraj taught this lesson to Class V every year, and the students liked it. Therefore, the lesson remained fresh in his mind. For the last twelve years, he had been repeating the moral and the humour of this lesson. His classes always enjoyed the story of the fox with the cut tail. He joined with his class in laughter at the story, but he presently controlled himself and said, "Don't make such a big noise. Do not laugh loudly. The headmaster's room is quite close. What if he hears you?"

Nandaraj took some satisfaction in his own method of teaching. With the ringing of the bell, he emerged from the class with a bright face.

The headmaster had called the teachers to a meeting. The subject of discussion was the lack of discipline among the boys. Nandaraj arrived at the headmaster's room. Some teachers had arrived earlier, while others were just arriving.

Everybody was grave, and each gave his opinion on the matter. The headmaster said, "The boys in our school lack discipline. They don't pay attention to their books. We are very much concerned about their studies. The examination results in the past four years have not been satisfactory."

Nandaraj remarked gravely, "This year, the results may be even worse. Perhaps, 30 percent, not more."

The headmaster didn't like Nandaraj's comment because he was just going to say the same thing. Nandaraj was always outspoken. He looked sharply at Nandaraj and resumed his own assessment of the situation.

Nandaraj was, however, elated by his own comment—it was mathematically correct. He would be surprised if the students did better than that! The teachers are not well informed about their students; they are only concerned about their own salaries.

Nandaraj spoke confidently, "It is not only in our school that the students have become undisciplined; it is the same elsewhere, too. It is the result of the international situation." He was very pleased at his own pronouncement. Who else has the brain to think so big? The headmaster tried to find out what the education department regulations said about it. He concluded that the lack of discipline among the boys was due to the erosion of the teachers' control over them. 'What narrow mindedness!' Nandaraj thought. 'He must have read about the psychology of boys when he did his B.T., and, yet, how could he have become so narrow minded?'

Nandaraj viewed his colleagues' rejection of his idea as a success for himself. He said to himself, 'They are just incapable of understanding it. They are afraid of fundamental principles, just as the mice are naturally afraid of the cat.'

The teachers, of course, accepted the headmaster's proposal. As soon as they emerged from the room, the drawing master said to Nandaraj, "Please come to my place this evening. I have invited some singers at 7.30. Let us have a pleasant time. I have also invited other teachers. You will have dinner, too."

Nandaraj accepted the invitation with pleasure. The drawing master was always amusing himself like this. Where did he get the money for such programmes? He has only 45 rupees, yet he wears a nice suit. If he was well-to-do, why would he be working for 45 rupees? He may be single, but that amount is nothing. Nor would anyone ask him to give private drawing lessons. With such questions in his mind, Nandaraj reached home and changed his clothes. When his wife brought him some sweetmeats, he looked with questioning eyes. "Umanath brought it," she explained. As he put the sweets into his mouth, he said to himself, 'Umanath is a gentle boy, bright enough in his studies, but I wonder what has gone wrong with him recently.'

In the evening, Nandaraj went to the drawing master's home. Quite a musical session was going on when he arrived, and the room resounded with the music of drums, harmonium[24] and *sitar*.[25] The room was filled with cigarette smoke. Everybody welcomed Nandaraj with great delight. The drum beats resumed, and the strings of the sitar wailed. Someone began to sing, "*piya bina ave nahin chaen.*" It was a Hindi song and meant, "There is no happiness without my beloved." The audience was thrilled.

Nandaraj stretched his arm and picked up a packet of cigarettes. He put a cigarette to his lips.

At the conclusion of the song, the singer put a *pan*[26] into his mouth and wiped the sweat from his face. The drawing

---

[24] A musical instrument played like a piano but operated by pumped air.

[25] A North Indian musical instrument with a long neck and a number of metal strings.

[26] Betel leaf.

master then pushed the harmonium in front of Nandaraj and said, "Please sing a song."

Nandaraj said quietly, "All right, but you first."

The host himself began a song. When he finished, the harmonium was again shifted to Nandaraj with a request, "Your turn." He deflected the request back to the host, repeating, "Yes, your turn." He said it in such a jocular manner that everybody laughed. Once again, Nandaraj avoided singing; he was pleased with his own cleverness and kept repeating, "Yes, your turn," as many times as his colleagues urged him to sing.

None of the teachers gathered in the room had a thought about the school. They forgot everything in the enjoyment of the moment. They had never smoked so many cigarettes before—in a chain, one after another. They clapped their hands, shook their heads, and "ahs" and "ohs" constantly came from their throats.

Nandaraj suddenly recalled the spirit and the enthusiasm of his college days, a spirit that he had taken as dead and gone. Now he was highly elated.

Finally, the music ceased, and everybody prepared for dinner. There was a scramble for the sweetmeats; the boys could not possibly have made as much commotion as the teachers did.

"Is this from Ram Bhandar?" Nandaraj asked.

Somebody answered him, "Where else can you get such good sweets?"

"No, it is not from Ram Bhandar," the host explained. "There is another shop. It looks small, but Ram Bhandar cannot compete with it in sweets."

All the teachers were taken by surprise. "Where is it?" they asked in one voice.

The dinner was over by 10.30 p.m., and everyone left for home.

Only a few men were to be seen in the streets. Nandaraj was suddenly sad. He was alone, and it was quite dark at various places. After the music and the dinner, he was depressed by the dark night. When he came home, he found the door bolted from within.

After he had knocked for a long time, the old maid servant came with a lantern and let him in. He went straight to his bedroom and found his wife asleep. He took off his clothes, pushed his wife aside and made room for himself. His wife muttered to herself and turned over close to the wall. Nandaraj got ample space for himself now. Sleep overcame him while he was still thinking of many things.

The Sweater

Woollen threads of different colours had come to the market. The shopkeepers replenished their stock of wool every November and displayed it attractively in showcases or hanging in their shops.

Mainya had bought some wool from the market. The colour of the wool was black with streaks of white. She wanted to knit a sweater for herself. While she was buying the wool, she thought of her own complexion and decided that this particular wool suited her. Black showed well against a fair complexion. The white streaks diminished the dark shade and added a nice touch to the wool. Mainya was very pleased with her choice of the wool.

After her meal, she sat down to knit her sweater. Her friends from the neighbourhood brought their own wool and needles and sat with her as they worked their needles. As the strands of wool gradually turned into different shapes and sizes, becoming sweaters, socks, gloves or jackets, the young women became talkative. Everyone was full of admiration for the wool Mainya had bought. "Where did you buy it?" they asked. "How much did it cost?"

They handled the wool by turn. They put their fingers through the material and examined the strands. Everyone exclaimed, "Yes, it is a very fine wool."

Mainya stopped her needles awhile and said, "This is available only in the Marwari's[27] shop, and everyone is buying it. If you like it, buy it at once."

A few minutes later, she put the sweater she had knitted, but for four inches, against her cheek and asked, "How does it look?"

---

[27] An Indian community known for remarkable business ability.

Everyone said in one voice, "Very pretty."

"We don't have your fair complexion," Bimala commented and looked at her own hands, turning them this way and that. "That wool won't do for my burnt skin."

Although Janaki openly stated her support for Bimala, she told herself that she would buy this particular kind of wool because, unlike Bimala, she did not hold a poor opinion of those with dark complexions.

After these comments, everyone kept working quietly. For a moment there was no sound in the room. Their fingers kept moving in and out, like serpents' tongues.

The silence was broken by Mainya herself with a question, "Eh, how many stitches?"

Janaki pretended not to know and asked deliberately, "For whom are you knitting the sweater? If he has a big belly, you will need more stitches. If he is lean, the number of stitches will be less. How can one say how many stitches are needed without knowing him. Tell me, who is that fortunate person?"

Mainya was angry with Janaki. She said sharply, "This Janaki is always joking in and out of season. I am making it for myself. Now, do you understand?"

The girls hardly suppressed their laughter.

Mainya had an afterthought: 'Perhaps, such a nice sweater should be given to someone. There is not much pleasure in making one for myself.'

When Janaki spoke again, there was no trace of a joke in her words. "If it is for you, 70 stitches will do, but you may go as many as 80."

Mainya kept on knitting. She made up her mind. She said to herself, 'Let me see how it will come out in the end, and then I'll decide.'

Harimaya, who had kept silent until then, said, "Oh, I don't know how to form the neck."

Bimala took the wool from Harimaya and began to knit the neck herself. Harimaya watched her with great attention.

Day by day, Mainya's sweater took shape. She had made up her mind. 'I'll give the sweater to Gajaraj,' she said to herself. 'He will be very pleased. He once asked me to knit a sweater for him. He said that he would love to wear a sweater made by my hand. So, Gajaraj shall have it. It will be a V-shaped one.'

As the sweater took shape, however, it appeared unattractive. It looked like a pillow case. Mainya was very distressed. It was not suitable to be given as a present. She could not even wear it herself. So, she gave it to Rame, the servant. As she gave it to him, she said, "Here, this is for you, Rame." The servant expressed his gratitude with a smile that brought wrinkles all over his face. She added, "I made it myself."

Mainya was very pleased to see Rame so happy. She had not worked in vain, she felt. There was, indeed, some satisfaction in giving something to someone like Rame. Gajaraj, too, would have been pleased if he had received the sweater, but his happiness would not be comparable to Rame's. When her friends met her the next time, they asked Mainya, "Who got that sweater?"

"I gave it to Rame," Mainya told them simply. "It was not good enough. Who else would wear something like that?"

But Janaki teased Mainya. "He is certainly fortunate to have your favour."

"Janaki, you are being too outspoken, "Mainya retorted furiously. "There is a limit to a joke."

But Janaki was not one to keep silent. She looked towards the other girls and said, "Did I say something wrong? I am only asking who is enjoying the fruits of Mainya's labour."

"Rame," everyone exclaimed at once.

Mainya was dumbfounded.

Thereafter, everyone came to know that Mainya had made a sweater herself and gave it to her servant. It became the talk in every home in the neighbourhood. The older people put their hands to their ears. "Oh, what did we have to hear!" they said to one another. Everyone took great interest in the matter and gave his or her opinion that Mainya's conduct was improper.

One day Mainya visited a friend in the neighbourhood. Her friend took Mainya aside where no one would see nor hear them and said, "People are talking about the sweater you made for Rame."

"So, what?" Mainya retorted.

Her friend explained, "Well, nothing has happened, but there is a rumour all around. If you had to give it to him, why didn't you do so without anyone's knowledge? Why did you have to beat your drum throughout the town?"

Mainya felt guilty for a moment. She tried to reason with her friend. "Well, was it wrong to give him a sweater?" she asked. "What can I do if people make something out of nothing. I cannot stop everyone's mouth."

"I didn't say you have done wrong," replied her friend. "I only said that you didn't do it cleverly enough. But I am a bit skeptical myself. Couldn't you find anyone else to give it to? Did you have to give it to a servant?"

Mainya was furious. "Isn't a servant a human being?" she shouted. "Would you dare to discriminate between master and servant in this age of equality? Well, since everyone says so, let it be so. To speak the truth, is love within anyone's control?"

Mainya was taken aback momentarily by her own vehement words. 'What did I say?' she asked herself. 'Love? Where did it come from, this word love?' But having roused herself to great anger, she was beyond caring. She continued, saying, "You know love does not care for anyone or anything. It is something given by God. It does not discriminate between the high and the low. The inner eye sees differently than the outer eye."

Her friend replied, "Mainya, you are angry. What you have said is true enough. The rules of our society are not recognized by true love. I do not say that Rame cannot be the object of your love because he is a servant. But there is something called 'face.' For me, it is the eighth wonder of the world that you see something in him. Also, he is older than you—at least 35—and you are no more than 21."

Mainya didn't like her friend's antiquated ideas. She said, "You don't know yet what love is. For you, love lies in riches, happiness and the gratification of the senses. For me, it is quite different. Do you understand now?"

With these words, Mainya left the place in a huff.

Knowing that their mistress was out, the servants were teasing Rame. "What more do you want now, Rame?" they said to him. "The mistress knitted a sweater with her own hands and gave it to you. Oh, fool, what do you make of it?"

In his embarrassment, Rame moved his hand over the sweater and merely kept grinning.

As she entered her room, Mainya overheard the servants. She didn't like them gathered there and their teasing of Rame. But she didn't dare to go then and there and scold the servants.

Love

"God has forgotten to open his eyes," Ramnath muttered to himself. "This rain is not going to stop. There is a drought in the Terai, and it is raining cats and dogs here, where there is no need for it." Ramnath began to have doubts about God's sagacity.

Rain or no rain, he had to go out. He put on his coat, picked up his umbrella and walked to the door. But, as if to mock him, at the same instant the rain intensified. The water from the roof ran in a stream in the gutter. The sky was dark. The sound of rain drops on the trees and on the tin roofs was monotonous. The street was deserted; not a single person was out. The rain made the trees in the neighbourhood bend low, and gusts of cold wind swept through the landscape, swirling drops of water along with it. Ramnath was dismayed; he felt very lonely.

But he had to go out anyway. He felt as if he should just disregard his work and stay home. He said to himself, 'Why do I have to go out on such a day? Why do I have to report to the office every day? How is our society set up? I have to work in spite of all the storms, while those in the big houses may sleep warmly through the bad weather, until their bodies ache from inaction. Such is the rule of the world! While the rich prosper, the poor must wear their bones out. It is said that there is no distinction between the rich and the poor in Russia. Can it be true? The source of all ills in society is the rich, none else. I don't remember where I have read this, but it is said that "the elephant will enter the eye of the needle before the rich get through the gateway to heaven."' In his resentment, Ramnath poured his wrath out on the rich.

Water was running in streams in the streets. There was mud everywhere. His shoes were becoming heavier, as the water soaked through and the mud stuck to the soles. It was even becoming difficult to walk. The rain lashed so heavily that the water penetrated his umbrella and fell, drop by drop, on his coat and cap. His patience was at an end by the time he got below Dhirdham.[28] 'Why was the municipality taking so long to repair this short stretch of road?' he said to himself. 'All the employees of the municipality are useless. They just know how to squeeze money out of the people. How efficient they are at collecting the tax but how slow in repairing even this short stretch of the road! Three days have passed since they dug up the road and barred all pedestrians from going this way. It is muddy everywhere. And how slippery! There is no proper arrangement of light nor a regular supply of water. Yet they call themselves the managers of the city!'

Arriving in his office, Ramnath turned on a lamp because there was not enough light. He folded the umbrella and kept it standing in a corner. A small lake was formed by the water that dropped from it. He shook his coat and hung it on a peg. Then he sat down and went through his papers. There was no work that needed his immediate attention, but the government rule is that because you are on a salary, you must be at your desk, whether there is work to be done or not. From the top to the bottom it was like this—a lack of wisdom in everything. It would not have made any difference if he had not come to the office on such a day. Oh, if he could leave this place and go somewhere else! It was better to die than be a slave like this.

For want of something to do, Ramnath sat with his chin resting on cupped hands and began to muse. Rama had written that she would come soon, but so far she had not. Once they are back in their natal home, women have no thought for their own home. June and July have gone, but she has no intention of returning. She used to write and say that she would be returning soon, but now the letters have

---

[28] A temple in the town of Darjeeling.

stopped coming. She has no love for her home, that's what it is. It is so long since a letter had come. From Monday to Monday, it is eight, Tuesday and Wednesday, make it ten days since her letter had come. Had she become ill? Ramnath rubbed his hands, got up from the chair and paced about the room. If she had fallen ill, her father should have written to him. These hill people may not even know that they ought to send notice when something went wrong. They never think much of an illness until it is serious. Because of such ignorance, many of our people die needlessly. Rama's health has not been good, either. She gets colds easily. And once she has a cold, she gets fever, cough and chest pains. Oh, how I wanted to take care of her, to have a good doctor examine and treat her! But I have not been able to, so far. Well, she is also to be blamed. She won't take the medicine that I get for her. Would any medicine taste nice? She ought to take care of herself, too. She didn't heed me when I told her not to eat hot, spicy and sour things. What can I do?

Ramnath's train of thought soon ran in another direction. I must dismiss the servant Rame. He never does a job well but talks big all the time. When I am alone, he disappears all day long. If he cleans the pots, he leaves oil stains all over. The Bahun also complains about Rame's work—the pots and dishes are not clean enough. As if the Bahun himself is a tidy fellow! How many times have I told Baje[29] to be neat and clean. I give him soap to wash himself, but his habits have not changed. He is always dirty. When she comes, I'll dismiss both of them and find new servants.

At the stroke of four o'clock, Ramnath got out of his chair, put on his coat, took his umbrella and came out of the office. The rain had stopped, but the sky was still full of clouds. All those people who had kept to their houses now

---

[29] Literally, grandfather, an honorific, Brahmin expression.

came out into the streets. Ramnath was tired. As soon as he reached home, he decided, he would get under a blanket and sleep. A friend was approaching from the opposite direction, and he wondered how long he was going to detain him.

The friend put his hand on Ramnath's shoulder and said, "Well, back from your office, Ramnath?"

He was angry. Everyone knew that Ramnath returned from his office at this hour. What was the need to ask the obvious?

The friend said again, "It rained the whole day." Ramnath's anger knew no bonds. Why did he have to keep standing in the middle of the road to engage in such silly talk? There was no need to remind Ramnath that it rained the whole day long. Sheer waste of time! Ramnath kept silent.

Finally, he was able to get rid of the friend and reach home. The servant took a long time to come and open the door. His anger knew no bounds, and he was about to strike the servant with the umbrella when he noticed a telegram lying on the table. He picked it up and hastily opened the envelope. It was from his wife, saying that she would be arriving on the following day.

The servant knew where the telegram had come from. He grinned and asked, "When is the mistress arriving?" Ramnath's mood at once became pleasant. "Tomorrow," he replied. "But before she arrives, tidy the house. What will she say? You have not swept the house since she left. Look, how dusty the table is." As he said so, he ran a finger across the table and showed the dust to the servant. With these words, he entered his room.

After a while, he called the servant. "Look," he said. "The almirah is standing in the middle. Let's keep it on one side of the room. It does not look nice now. The table and the chair should be placed close to the top of the bed. You get hold of one end, but be careful."

During supper, Ramnath said to the Bahun, "Get some meat tomorrow. Why do you buy only one kind of vegetables? Isn't there anything else?"

The next morning, Ramnath discovered that his body was very light and he was full of energy. The sky was cloudless. The sun was like liquid gold all over the hills. In a very happy mood, he called the servant, "Rame, what time does the train come?"

"Is she coming by train?" the servant asked. "She would arrive sooner if she came by car."

Ramnath was nonplused. If she came by car, where was he to go to receive her? She could have mentioned it in the telegram. He racked his brains for a moment and then said to Rame, "You go and stay on the road. If she doesn't come by car, I'll go to the railway station. The train comes at 12 o'clock, isn't it so?"

"Yes, sir," the servant replied.

As the servant was about to go, Ramnath said, "Keep some fresh flowers in the pot. You have no common sense. You have kept the flowers rotting for seven days."

He entered the kitchen and asked the Bahun, "What vegetables did you bring, Baje? You may cook somewhat late today. If she comes by train, it won't be before 12 o'clock. For once you may be late. What's the use of letting the food go cold?"

After he had taken his bath, Ramnath stood in the middle of the room for a while and asked himself, "What shall I do now?"

He put on his coat and walked towards the road along which the car would come. Rame was sitting upon a stone by the road side, and seeing his master approach, he stood up.

"Hasn't she come yet?" he asked.

"A number of cars have come," Rame replied, "but she hasn't."

Ramnath stood still for awhile, and concluding that she was not coming by car, sent the servant home. "Look here," he said. "Come to the railway station with the umbrella and raincoat. I'll stay here for a while."

Ramnath cast his eyes upwards. There were signs of rain. The clouds were beginning to gather again. He made his way to the railway station. There was nobody yet. The clerks were busy in their office. The platform was empty. He sat down on a bench for some time. Then he wandered about on the platform. He read the advertisements on the wall, one by one. '*The Statesman* is the national daily with the greatest circulation in India. Read it if you want to keep in contact with the world.' 'Horlicks is an energy giving drink. Give Horlicks to small children and the sick.' There was a picture of a very healthy looking old man with rosy cheeks. Ramnath concluded that it was an advertisement for Wake's beer. Ramnath proceeded towards the clock to see if his watch was correct. He found his watch was fast by five minutes. Once more he paced about the platform before sitting down on the bench.

Gradually, people began to arrive at the station. The bell rang. It was time for the train to arrive. He got up from the bench. Rame came with the umbrella and rain coat. Just then the train came in. Ramnath's eyes at once caught sight of his wife, who had her head out of the train window. He went towards her, and she stepped down. Leaving the servant to bring the luggage, the couple walked out of the station. It began to rain heavily at the same time. Ramnath put on the rain coat and held the umbrella over his wife. "Look," he said. "It is raining to welcome you home." He waxed poetic and added, "There was no rain until you arrived. How nicely the rain is timed to coincide with your arrival!" Ramnath found correct the saying that rain is auspicious.

"Come under the umbrella," said Ramnath. "You will get wet. Don't hurry. The road is very slippery. Look, they are making the road wider because it has become narrow. They are going to widen it by three more cubits. They have dug up the earth there. Is this great road going to be complete in just a few days? No, it may take a fortnight or more to make it. The men are working day and night. Be careful, you will slip on the road. Here, hold my hand."

Ramnath suddenly burst into laughter when his wife slipped in the mud. The next moment he found himself on the ground. The umbrella fell from his hand, skipped along the road and rested against a fence. His wife also laughed. "What a big fish!" she cried, but the next moment she was anxious. "You aren't hurt, are you?"

Ramnath got to his feet and said, "No, I am not hurt, but did anyone see us?" His wife looked around. There was no one about. She locked her hand into her husband's and went down the slope.

Upon reaching home, his wife checked the luggage that the porter had carried. The servant stood by the door with a grin on his face. She asked, "Was Rame good in his job?"

The servant's grin became wider, showing all his teeth, when Ramnath said with a smile, "He did quite well. He managed everything. Only I don't know how he got lost during the nights." With a wink, he looked at his wife.

The rain was pouring outside. The servant went to the kitchen. The wife prepared herself to take a bath. She opened a box and took out her clothes. Ramnath stood close by her, and she asked, "Don't you have to go to the office today?"

"Well, who will go today, not me," Ramnath said, as he tapped his fingers on his wife's head as if he were playing upon the keys of the harmonium.

His wife went to take her bath. Ramnath sat down on the bed.

The sound of water being poured from a jug reached him every now and then. His cup of happiness was full to the brim.

PBH
OTHER WORKS BY KESAR LALL
FROM PILGRIMS BOOK HOUSE

Anecdotes and Stories of the Gurkha Soldier

Who hasn't heard of Nepal's most famous representatives, the fearless Gurkha soldier? Here is a collection of delightful anecdotes and stories about the legendary Gurkha. As one soldier states: "They feared us, but all said and done, if we can win by reputation, who wants to kill people?"
70 pages. Paperback. B&W illustrations.
US $2.75 Item No. 50. Shipping: Sea/Air $.50/$1.50

Lore and Legend of Nepal

Giants and demons, Bungadeo, the God of Mercy, and Bandhu Achaju, the Tantric Master, feature in thirty-one traditional folktales from Nepal. Entertaining and illuminating reading. "Even people of sophisticated tastes will enjoy" - Times of India.
73 pages. Paperback. B&W illustrations.
US $2.75 Item No: 025. Shipping: Sea/Air $ 0.50/$1.50

Nepalese Book of Proverbs

Proverbs are very much used in Nepal and, while the proverbs are of universal application, they also preserve the distinct flavour of the Nepalese land and its people. Here are 447 proverbs on every subject from "the rich and the poor" to "fire, wind and water" to "sin, sorrow, fear and folly". Each proverb is quoted in its original Nepali or Newari language and, on the facing page, its English translation.
98 pages. Paperback.
US $2.75 Item No: 026 Shipping: Sea/Air $0.50/$1.50

Pilgrims Proverbs from the Animal Kingdom

Man's use of different animals for the purpose of instructing his own kind through tales, fables and proverbs makes a fascinating subject. This book features many little known animal proverbs from across the world, arranged alphabetically from "ant" to "yak".
71 pages. Paperback. B&W illustrations.
US $2.25   Item No: 040. Shipping: Sea/Air $0.50/$1.50

Pilgrims Proverbs of Nepal and Other Countries

The proverb is part of folklore that is more basic than the folktale or the folksong. It gives us a peep into mankind's thinking and way of life in the centuries gone by. Its meaning is still not lost and is often subtle and sophisticated in meaning. This collection contains five hundred proverbs, one fifth of them from Nepal.
55 pages. Paperback. B&W illustrations.
US $1.25   Item No: 028. Shipping: Sea/Air $0..50/$1.50

Lore and Legend of the Yeti

"Yeti Footprints Sighted Again", "Yeti Is Not A Myth", "Another Yeti Expedition": so cry the world's newspaper headlines year in year out. Kesar Lall recounts the fascinating chronicles of the reported sightings of the Snowman and the numerous expeditions mounted to locate him. He reveals the existence of the Yeti in Sherpa folklore and the reports of similar (or the same?) wildmen in other lands. One expedition leader mused: "Inscrutable Snowman...perhaps thou art yet to be found in remotest mountains of Nepal. Perhaps!"
89 pages. Paperback. B&W line drawings.
US $1.25   Item No: 002. Shipping: Sea/Air $0.50/$1.50

Tales of the Yeti

These nine tales concern the Yeti, the wildman known in the West as the Abominable Snowman. They were collected by the author in the course of his travels in different parts of northern Nepal.
24 pages. Paperback. B&W illustrations.
US $.40   Item No: 005. Shipping: Sea/Air $0.50/$1.50

The Pilgrims Quotations from the Buddhist Scriptures

Buddhism needs no introduction to the rest of the world now, but Kesar Lall skillfully extracts meaningful scriptures of the Theravada tradition in order to help the reader and visitor to better understand the people of Nepal through their religious beliefs and way of life.
63 pages. Booklet. B&W drawings.
US $2.75 Shipping: Sea/Air $0.50/$1.50

A Hymn By Rana Bahadur Shah
Translated by Kesar Lall

This 18th century king of Nepal married out of caste a woman with whom he was madly in love. His was a great love, such as only a poet would dream of. This hymn was written in memory of his beloved queen. Newari script, transliteration and word for word translation into English.
50 pages. Booklet.
US $2.25   Item No. 53. Shipping: Sea/Air $0.50/$2.00

The Pilgrims Proverbs About Man and Woman

Of proverbs on various subjects, there are none of greater interest than those about the mind of man and woman. "The mind may be grasped but not easily described." Yet, this collection of proverbs from Nepal and other countries is a delightful introduction.
49 pages. Booklet.
US $1.95 Shipping: Sea/Air $ 0.50/$1.50

Love Songs From Nepal

Love lurks in every human heart, and as a theme of literature, it is of endless interest to all peoples. This is no less true of the Newars, who are better known for their religious fervour, which they express with great skill in stone, wood and metal. A large number of poems, plays and songs have been preserved in the oral tradition and in handwritten manuscripts, and many of these have appeared in print in recent years. A subtle sense of the beauty and joy of life, as well as the enthusiasm and optimism of young men and women, permeate these songs that span the last five centuries.

These and other fine titles may be ordered by mail. Bank drafts or credit card orders accepted by fax with card number, expiration date and signature. Request our free publication catalogue. Publishing inquires welcomed.

PILGRIMS BOOK HOUSE
Kathmandu ♦ Lalitpur ♦ Varanasi

Head Office: Thamel, P.O. Box 3872, Kathmandu, Nepal
Fax: 977-1-424943. E-mail: info@pilgrims.wlink.com.np
Web Site: http://gfas.com/pilgrims